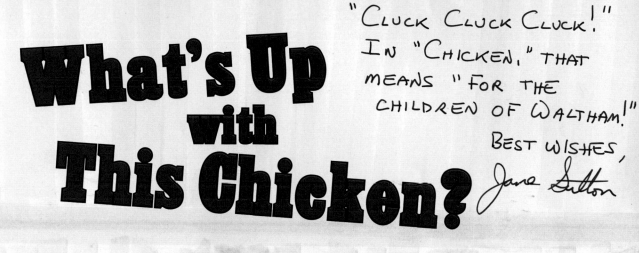

What's Up with This Chicken?

By Jane Sutton

Illustrated by Peter J. Welling

"CLUCK CLUCK CLUCK!"
IN "CHICKEN," THAT
MEANS "FOR THE
CHILDREN OF WALTHAM!"
BEST WISHES,
Jane Sutton

PELICAN PUBLISHING COMPANY
GRETNA 2015

The word "Pelican" and the depiction of a pelican are trademarks of Pelican Publishing Company, Inc., and are registered in the U.S. Patent and Trademark Office.

Library of Congress Cataloging-in-Publication Data

Sutton, Jane.
  What's up with this chicken? / by Jane Sutton ; illustrated by Peter J. Welling.
      pages cm
  Summary: "Backyard chickens usually give families nice, fresh eggs, but not Trudy. She won't get off her eggs, and she pecks Sylvia and Grandma when they try to reach under her! When the resourceful Sylvia discovers the answer, she gains new respect for stubborn Trudy and comes up with an 'egg-cellent' solution"– Provided by publisher.
  ISBN 978-1-4556-2085-2 (hardcover : alk. paper) – ISBN 978-1-4556-2086-9 (e-book) [1. Chickens—Fiction. 2. Eggs—Fiction. 3. Mother and child—Fiction.] I. Welling, Peter J., illustrator. II. Title.
  PZ7.S96824Wj 2015
  [Fic]—dc23
                                                                2014049830

Printed in Malaysia
Published by Pelican Publishing Company, Inc.
1000 Burmaster Street, Gretna, Louisiana 70053

*For my fabulous friend Fay, who inspired this book
—J. S.*

*We have an empty nest now but there are a lot of
good eggs in my family. Here's to Darlene, Shawn,
Justin, Michael, Andy, Mary, Heather, Missy, Christina,
Kyle, Kasen, Kara, Jacy, David, and Matty, who help to
keep me crowing.—P. J. W.*

SUE   TRUDY   DO

Something was up with Trudy. She wouldn't let Sylvia take her egg. When Sylvia reached under Trudy, Trudy squawked and screeched. "Don't get so *egg-cited!*" Sylvia told Trudy. "I'll get your egg tomorrow."

SUE

TRUDY

DORIS

But the next day, when Sylvia reached for Trudy's egg, Trudy tried to peck her! Sylvia was *not* pleased with Trudy. "What's up with this chicken?" she wondered. Sylvia wished Trudy would act like the other chickens in Grandma's backyard.

Sue cleaned her feathers at least ten times a day.

Doris ate everything in sight—chicken feed, grass, ants, and caterpillars.

Olga took dozens of dust baths that sent up clouds of dirt.

Clara raced around in circles and cluck-cluck-clucked.

The other hens all let Sylvia collect their eggs. But Trudy refused. "This is getting *egg-stremely* annoying," thought Sylvia.

Grandma was cooking omelets with eggs from Sue, Clara, Doris, and Olga. Sylvia told her about stubborn Trudy and asked, "What's up with this chicken?"

"I don't know," said Grandma. "Trudy has always let us take her eggs before." Grandma gave Sylvia an omelet and a kiss on top of her head. "Try again tomorrow," she said.

But the next day, when Sylvia reached for an egg, Trudy squawked, screeched, and tried to peck Sylvia again. Trudy puffed herself up to twice her size.

Sylvia noticed that Trudy left her roost just once a day to eat, drink, and poop. She was getting skinny.

Sylvia figured Trudy had to be hungry! "Come get this delicious chicken feed," she said. (The chicken feed didn't *really* look delicious, but all the other hens wolfed it down like chocolate.)

Trudy wasn't tempted by the chicken feed. She just stayed on her roost, sitting on her eggs.

Sylvia tried frightening Trudy off her eggs. "Oh no, Trudy!" she said. "There's a huge snake under you...."
Squawk! Screech! Puff! Peck!
"This is getting *eggs-asperating*," thought Sylvia.

But Sylvia was not about to give up. . . . She looked in her box of Halloween costumes for the scariest mask she could find. With the mask on, Sylvia stomped up to Trudy's roost, waved her arms, and yelled, *"Whaaah!"* Trudy didn't budge.

"Why aren't you scared?" Sylvia asked Trudy. "I thought chickens were chicken!"

That night Sylvia asked Grandma again, "What's up with this chicken?"

Grandma got out her big book called *The Big Book About Chickens.* She turned to the table of contents. "Aha!" said Grandma, after reading a little further.

"Why are you aha-ing?" asked Sylvia. "Does it say what's up with this chicken?"

"It does," answered Grandma. "Trudy is broody!" Grandma read from the book: "Broody hens stay on their eggs so they will hatch into chicks."

"But our hens lay the kind of eggs you eat, not the baby-chicken kind," said Sylvia.

"You're right," said Grandma. "Trudy can sit on those eggs all day and all night, but they won't turn into chicks."

"I guess we should call her Broody Trudy!" said Sylvia.

"I think so, too," said Grandma, giggling. Sylvia loved Grandma's giggle.

Sylvia started thinking about Broody Trudy. No wonder she didn't act like the other chickens. She wanted to be a mother! But she couldn't because her eggs didn't have chicks inside.

Sylvia wished she could help Trudy. She thought and thought.

"Maybe . . . maybe, yes!" said Sylvia. "Grandma, can we get eggs that *will* hatch?"

"What a good idea!" said Grandma.

"I think you mean an *egg-cellent* idea," said Sylvia.

Grandma giggled. "I'll send away for eggs that will hatch!" she said, hugging Sylvia.

A few days later, a box arrived from Eggs Eggs-press. Inside were four eggs.

Grandma and Sylvia headed out to the chicken coop. Sylvia carried her egg-collecting basket and the box from Eggs Eggs-press. Grandma put on thick gloves that went up to her elbows.

Grandma lifted Trudy from her roost. Trudy squawked and flapped and pecked so much that Grandma put her back down. Sylvia was glad Grandma was wearing thick gloves!

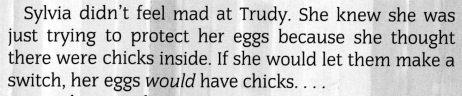

Sylvia didn't feel mad at Trudy. She knew she was just trying to protect her eggs because she thought there were chicks inside. If she would let them make a switch, her eggs *would* have chicks. . . .

Grandma tried again. *Squawk! Flap! Peck! Screech!* For such a skinny chicken, Trudy sure was strong.

SUE

TRUDY

DO

Grandma put Trudy down and took a deep breath. "Let's try again," she said. "Ready?"

Sylvia took a deep breath, too. "Ready!" she said.

Grandma lifted Trudy. Again, Trudy puffed herself up, squawked, flapped, and pecked. But Grandma held on.

As quickly and carefully as she could, Sylvia took away the three eggs Trudy had been sitting on and replaced them with the four eggs from the box.
Broody Trudy settled down on the new eggs.

Sylvia and Grandma waited—and waited and waited.
Every day, Sylvia collected eggs from Sue, Clara, Doris, and Olga.
Broody Trudy kept sitting on her new eggs. She left her roost just once a day to eat, drink, and poop. Sylvia thought she looked skinnier every day.

Sometimes Broody Trudy rolled the eggs to make sure they were warm all over. She even pulled off some of her chest feathers to make a blanket for the eggs!

One day, Sylvia heard peeping. She called Grandma out to the coop.

Chicks!

Beneath Broody Trudy's feathers, Sylvia and Grandma saw three wet-looking, tiny, peeping chicks. Pieces of shell stuck to them. The fourth chick was still pecking its way out.

TRUDY

Soon the chicks were dry. Sylvia and Grandma named the little yellow fluff balls Sophie, Danielle, Mildred, and Judy.

When the chicks took their first steps, Broody Trudy finally got up from her roost.

Sylvia thought she would head straight for the chicken feed. Instead she walked around the backyard with her wings spread over her chicks. Sylvia thought Trudy looked like a feathery beach umbrella.

Trudy wouldn't go anywhere without Sophie, Danielle, Mildred, and Judy.

She taught them to gobble chicken feed as if it were chocolate.

She taught them to sip water at the trough.

She taught them to scratch in the dirt for bug and caterpillar snacks.

She taught them to roll in the dust to get clean.

"Broody Trudy is an awesome mother!" said Sylvia.
"I agree!" said Grandma.
"Or do you *egg-gree?*" Sylvia asked, making Grandma giggle.
Now Trudy ate lots of chicken feed. She wasn't skinny anymore.

As the chicks got older, they turned different colors. They no longer fit under Trudy's wings. But she still watched over them.

After a while, the chicks' peep-peep-peeps became deep cluck-cluck-clucks.

And a long time after that, Trudy's chickens laid eggs of their own!

One day, Sylvia collected an egg from Sophie, an egg from Danielle, and two from Mildred.

But when she reached under Judy . . . Judy wouldn't let Sylvia take her egg. She puffed herself up and squawked and screeched and pecked.

Sylvia laughed so hard that she almost dropped her egg basket. "Broody Judy," she said, "I know what's up with you!"

Author's Note

My friend Fay, with an armful of chickens

As soon as my friend Fay told me about the odd behavior of her favorite backyard chicken, Raven, and the reasons behind it, I knew I had to write a book about it. Raven, a beautiful and sweet-natured hen, suddenly began sitting on her eggs all day. While the other hens left their eggs to scratch for bugs in the yard, Raven stayed put in her roost.

So Fay asked a chicken expert and learned about broody hens. I had always thought that "broody" meant worried or gloomy. But in hens, it refers to a kind of super-maternal drive to sit on eggs so that they hatch into chicks. However, the eggs that chickens lay for eating are not "fertilized," so they will never hatch.

Broody hens leave their nests just once a day to eat, drink, and take care of business. And some (not the good-natured Raven) can put up a fight if someone tries to take their eggs! Broody hens often develop "brood patches" on their chests, from plucking out their own feathers to keep the eggs warm.

Like Sylvia and Grandma in *What's Up with This Chicken?* Fay ordered fertilized eggs. And when they hatched, Fay was delighted to discover that Raven, like Trudy, was a wonderful mother!

In writing my story, I included facts and added characters with a problem to solve and lots of chicken puns. I hope readers will enjoy the story of Trudy, who at first annoys Sylvia with her stubbornness. But the determined hen wins Sylvia's sympathy and admiration, as she learns that Broody Trudy is being difficult for a good reason.